Rookie reader®

Shoelaces

By
Suzanne Lieurance

Illustrated by
Patrick Girouard

Children's Press®
A Division of Grolier Publishing
New York • London • Hong Kong • Sydney
Danbury, Connecticut

For Adrian, Nicholas, and Tyler—
tied together like the best of shoelaces.
—S. L.

For Rebecca, Joe, and Aunt Mary.
—P. G.

Reading Consultants
Linda Cornwell
Coordinator of School Quality and Professional Improvement
(Indiana State Teachers Association)

Katharine A. Kane
Education Consultant
(Retired, San Diego County Office of Education and San Diego State University)

Visit Children's Press® on the Internet at:
http://publishing.grolier.com

Library of Congress Cataloging-in-Publication Data
Lieurance, Suzanne.
    Shoelaces / by Suzanne Lieurance ; illustrated by Patrick Girouard.
        p.   cm. — (Rookie reader)
    Summary: A child describes the joys of all different kinds of shoelaces.
    ISBN 0-516-21613-9 (lib.bdg.)   0-516-26546-6 (pbk.)
    [1. Shoelaces Fiction. 2. Stories in rhyme.] I. Girouard, Patrick, ill.
II. Title. III. Series.
PZ8.3.L598Sh 2000   99-23554
                                                                    CIP

GROLIER
PUBLISHING 1 2 3 4 5 6 7 8 9 10 R 09 08 07 06 05 04 03 02 01 00

I like shoelaces.

I can tie my shoes.

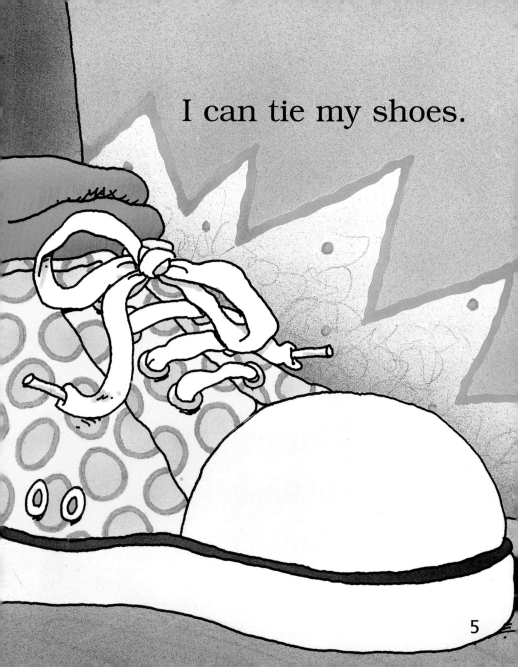

It doesn't really matter.
Any lace will do.

7

8

Short laces, long laces,
laces just right.

I make a bow
and tie it up tight.

11

12

Bright laces, striped laces,
one to a shoe.

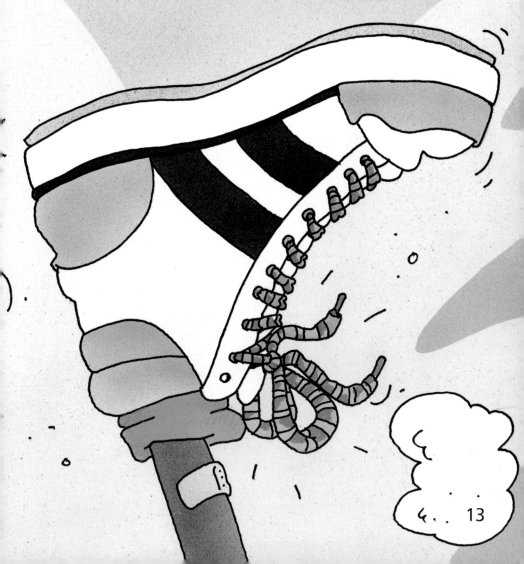

Round laces, flat laces, smooth laces, too!

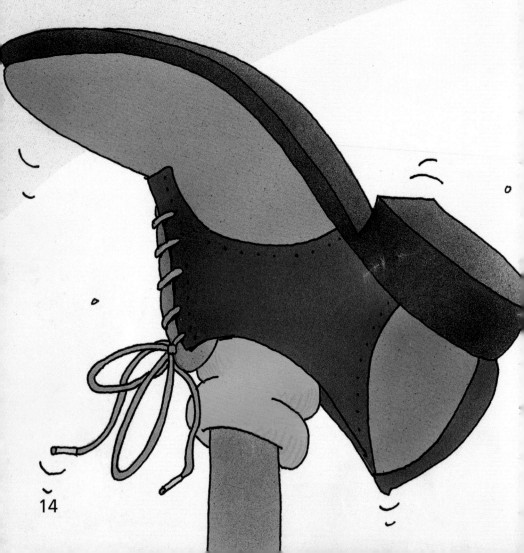

Red laces, blue laces,
pulled through my shoe.

Plain laces, fancy laces,
any kind will do.

Boys' laces, girls' laces,
laces with my name.

21

When tied in a bow,
they all work the same.

I like
shoelaces.

Any kind will do.

Oops! Laces came undone.

29

Time to tie my shoe!

Word List (58 words)

a	do	lace	plain	short	to
all	doesn't	laces	pulled	smooth	too
and	fancy	like	really	striped	undone
any	flat	long	red	the	up
blue	girls'	make	right	they	when
bow	I	matter	round	through	will
boys'	in	my	same	tie	with
bright	it	name	shoe	tied	work
came	just	one	shoelaces	tight	
can	kind	oops	shoes	time	

About the Author

Suzanne Lieurance is a former teacher, now a full-time freelance writer. Besides writing books for children, she also writes a monthly online column for children's writers (www.wordmuseum.com/childrencolumn.htm) and many of her articles and stories have been published in a variety of magazines, newspapers, and ezines. Suzanne lives in Kansas City, Missouri, with her husband and two sons.

About the Illustrator

Patrick Girouard learned to tie laces from his sweet Aunt Mary. He loves canvas hightop sneakers, dogs, sidewalk chalk, coffee, movies, bagels with everything, books, and drawing (not necessarily in that order). He has two sons called Marc and Max, and they all live in Indiana.